This 123 sticker activity book belongs to:

....

1 **one**

Can you put a sunflower sticker in the vase?

Here is a doghouse. Can you find
one dog sticker to put inside?

1
2
3
4
5
6
7
8
9
10

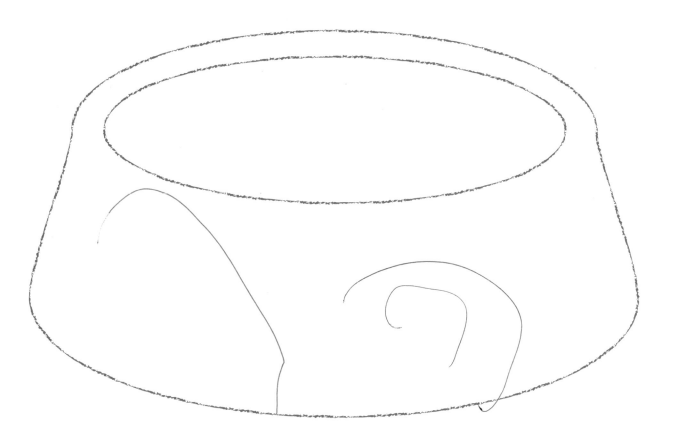

This is a dog bowl. Add some color and decorate it with your stickers.

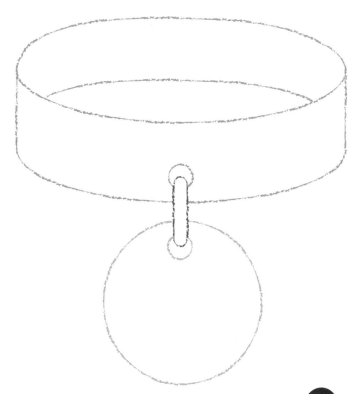

This is a dog collar. Can you color it in? You could even give your dog a name and write it on the tag.

1
2
3
4
5
6
7
8
9
10

5

Find one wheel for the unicycle on the sticker pages.

Find one hat for the scarecrow on the sticker pages.

Color and decorate the numeral one and the word one!

1

2 two

2

Using your stickers, can you add two swans swimming on the river?

3

4

How many boats are on the river?

5

6

7

8

9

10

How many helicopters
are in the sky?

1
2
3
4
5
6
7
8
9
10

Color in this pair of boots!

Trace the two wiggly shoelaces!

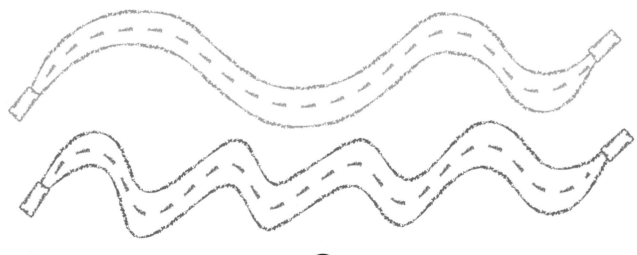

Using your crayons, can you give these butterflies wings?

These pairs of shoes are all mixed up! Draw a line from the shoe on the left to its match on the right. How many shoes are in each pair?

Color and decorate the numeral two and the word two!

3 three

These three bears are all very hungry! Can you find three jars of honey on the sticker pages?

1
2
3
4
5
6
7
8
9
10

14

Add three pieces of fruit to this fruit bowl using the stickers.

Can you find three flower stickers for the bees to land on?

Color in these three little pigs!

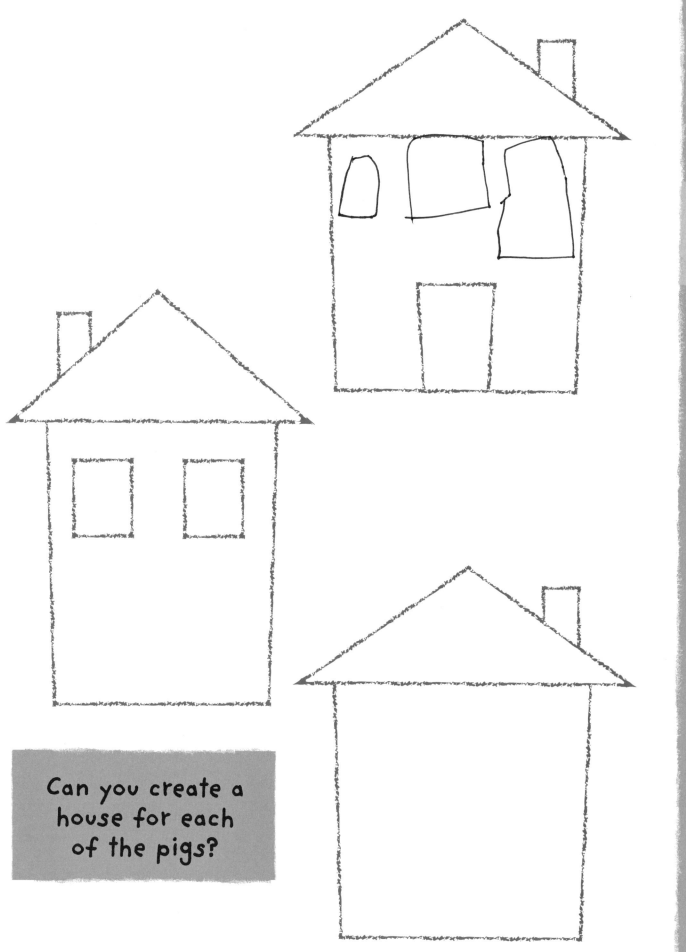

Can you create a
house for each
of the pigs?

1
2
3
4
5
6
7
8
9
10

17

Can you color in these three candies?

1
2
3
4
5
6
7
8
9
10

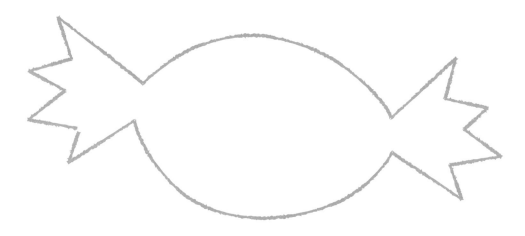

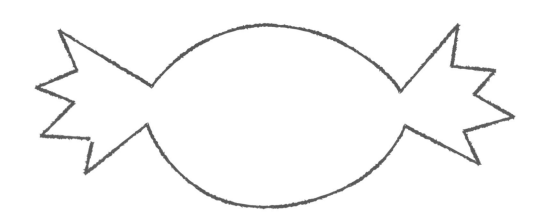

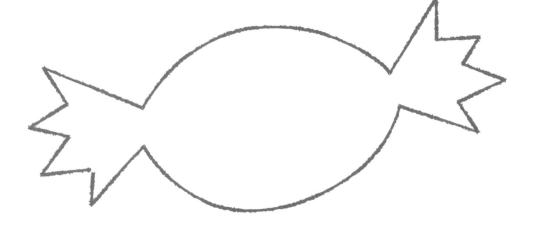

Color and decorate the numeral three and the word three!

1
2
3
4
5
6
7
8
9
10

1
2
3
4
5
6
7
8
9
10

4 four

Freddie is four years old today! Add four sticker candles to his birthday cake.

How many party hats are there? How many party blowers are there?

Can you draw four black spots on each of these ladybugs?

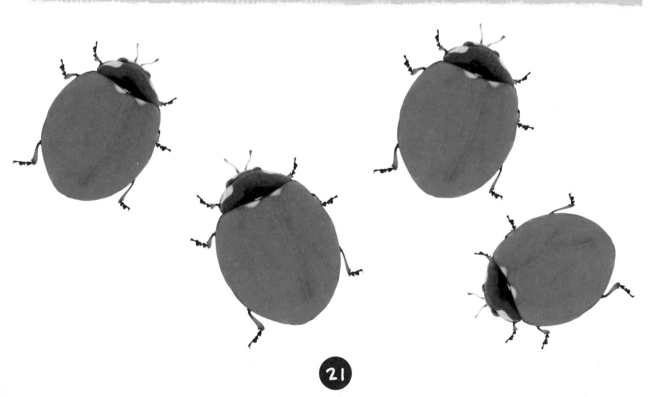

1

2

3

4

5

6

7

8

9

10

Trace the dotted lines to reveal four furry friends.

Color in these four birthday presents.

Find the missing balloon stickers, then count the balloons!

Color and decorate the numeral four and the word four!

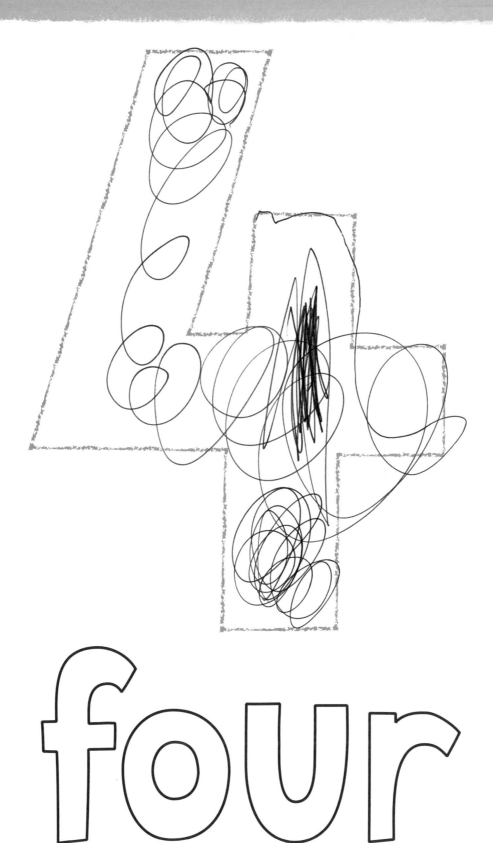

1
2
3
4
5
6
7
8
9
10

1
2
3
4
5
6
7
8
9
10

5 five

A baby pig is called a piglet. Can you add five piglet stickers to the scene?

Trace your hand in the frame and color it in.
How many fingers do you have?

Five little speckled frogs sat on a speckled log, eating the most delicious bugs. Can you add five frog stickers to this log and draw some bugs?

Trace the dotted lines to draw five red apples hanging on the branch.
Now color them in!

How many flowers are there?

1
2
3
4
5
6
7
8
9
10

Can you find five monkey stickers
and add them to the palm tree?

30

Color and decorate the numeral
five and the word five!

1
2
3
4
5
6
7
8
9
10

6 six

Can you find six egg stickers to fill in the empty carton?

How many buns are there? Which one is different?

Can you draw six lollipop tops on these sticks?

1
2
3
4
5
6
7
8
9
10

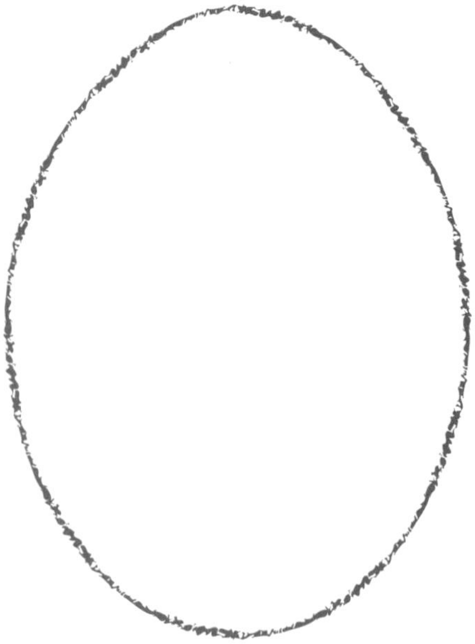

Decorate
these
six eggs
using your
crayons.

Can you trace the swirly shells on these six snails?

1
2
3
4
5
6
7
8
9
10

Can you find **six** bird stickers and add them to their perch?

Color and decorate the numeral six and the word six!

1

2

3

4

5

6

7

8

9

10

1
2
3
4
5
6
7
8
9
10

7 seven

How many ballet dancers are on the stage?

Add petals to these **seven** circles to make pretty flowers.

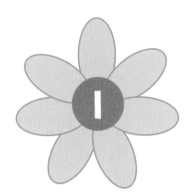

2

4

6

7

Draw seven portholes on this boat!

Find seven squirrel stickers and add them to this tree.

1

2

3

4

5

6

7

8

9

10

Can you find **seven** button stickers for this coat?

Color and decorate the numeral seven and the word seven!

seven

1

2

3

4

5

6

7

8

9

10

1
2
3
4
5
6
7
8
9
10

8 eight

Polly the parrot has found a treasure chest. How many gold coins are in the treasure chest?

Octopuses have eight arms.
Use your crayons to color in the octopus.

1
2
3
4
5
6
7
8
9
10

1
2
3
4
5
6
7
8
9
10

Draw eight bugs in the spider web.

1
2
3
4
5
6
7
8
9
10

1

2

3

4

5

6

7

8

9

Can you add **eight** star stickers
to the night sky?

10

Color and decorate the numeral eight and the word eight!

8

eight

1
2
3
4
5
6
7
8
9
10

49

q nine

This cat lost her nine kittens. Help her through the maze to bring her kittens home. Can you count the kittens?

1
2
3
4
5
6
7
8
9
10

1
2
3
4
5
6
7
8
9
10

Add nine gem stickers to this royal crown.

Using your crayons, color in the **nine** jewels.

52

The edible part of a carrot grows underground. Can you find nine carrot stickers and add them to this scene?

1
2
3
4
5
6
7
8
9
10

Look at these yummy cupcakes!
Use the stickers to decorate them.

1
2
3
4
5
6
7
8
9
10

Color and decorate the numeral nine and the word nine!

9

nine

1
2
3
4
5
6
7
8
9
10

1
2
3
4
5
6
7
8
9
10

10 ten

This rocket ship is missing its windows. Can you add ten window stickers to it?

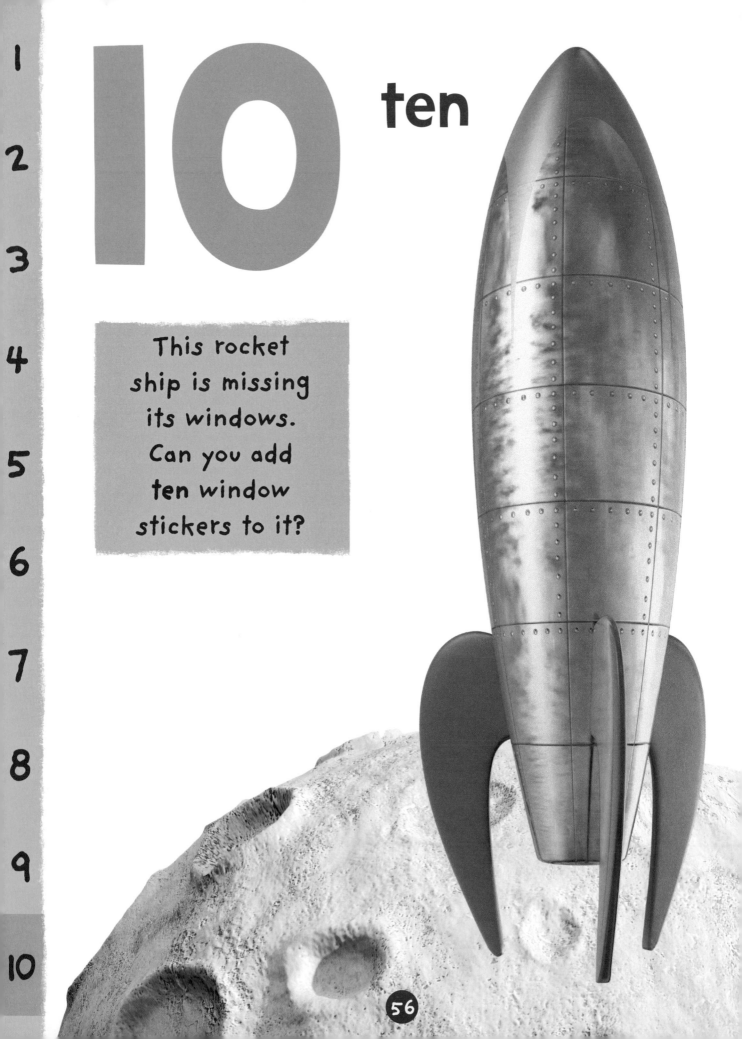

Turn these ten circles into aliens. Draw arms and legs and add some eye stickers.

1
2
3
4
5
6
7
8
9
10

Can you follow the lines to lead the puppies to their dog food?

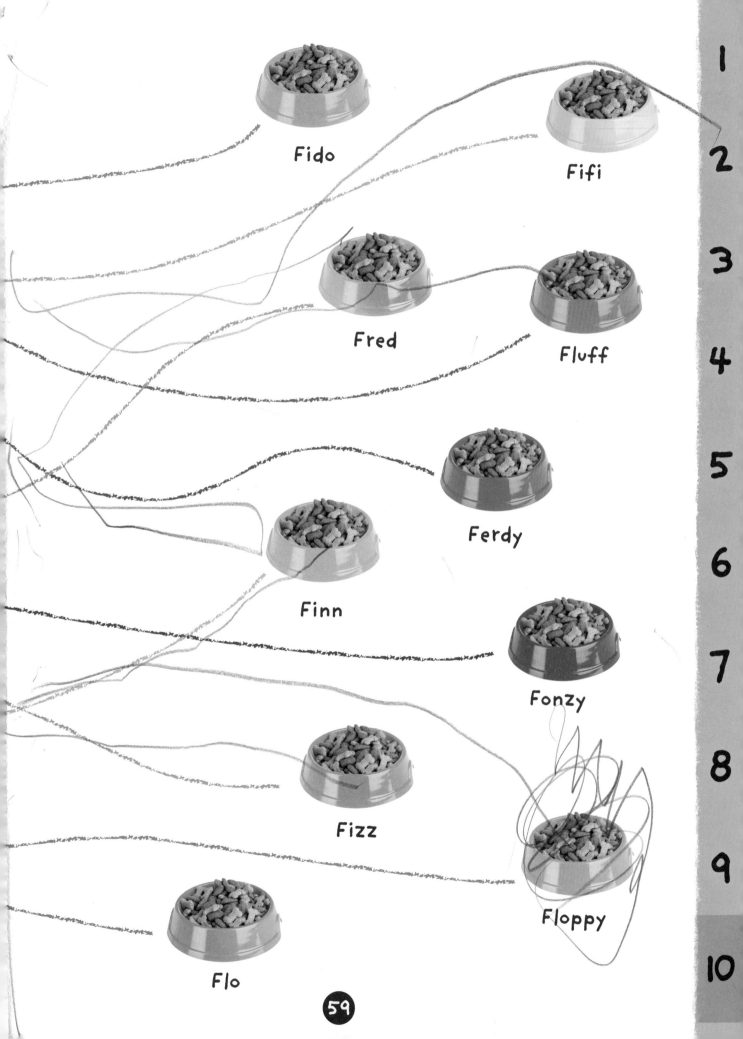

Fido

Fifi

Fred

Fluff

Ferdy

Finn

Fonzy

Fizz

Floppy

Flo

1
2
3
4
5
6
7
8
9
10

59

Can you find **ten** teddy bears on the sticker pages and add them to the bed?

Can you count how many fingers are in this pair of gloves? Use your crayons to color them in.

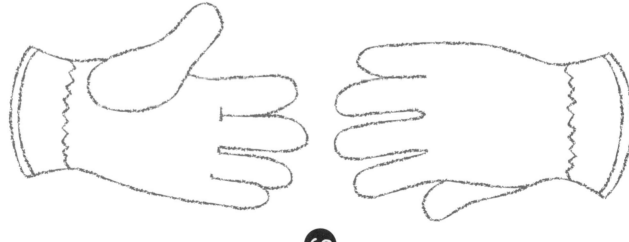

Color and decorate the numeral ten and the word ten!

ten

1
2
3
4
5
6
7
8
9
10

Find ten fish stickers for this aquarium.

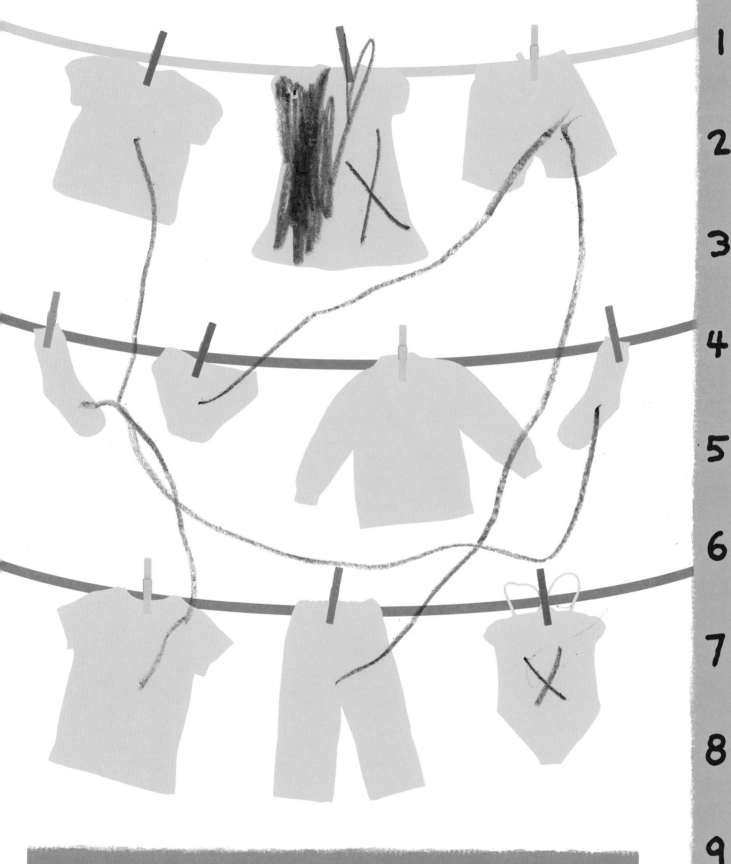

Can you find the stickers for the ten pieces of clothing hanging on the clothesline?

1
2
3
4
5
6
7
8
9
10

Find the sum of the numbers and place the correct sticker to answer each question. Use the objects underneath the numbers to help you.

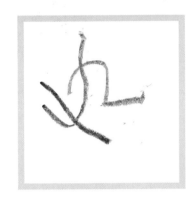

Color in the numbers from one to ten.

1
2
3
4
5
6
7
8
9
10

1 Trace one flower!

2 Trace two circles!

3 Trace three squares!

4 Trace four spirals!

5 Trace five dots!

6

Trace
six
triangles!

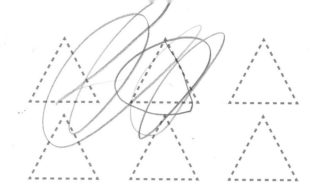

7

Trace
seven
rectangles!

8

Trace
eight
hearts!

9

Trace
nine
droplets!

10

Trace
ten
stars!

1
2
3
4
5
6
7
8
9
10

There are

....

feathers.

There are

....

crayons.

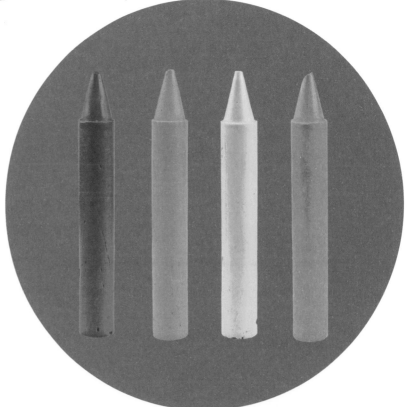

1
2
3
4
5
6
7
8
9
10

There are

....

eggs.

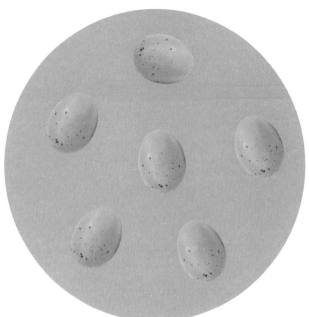

There are

....

gloves.

There are

....

buttons.

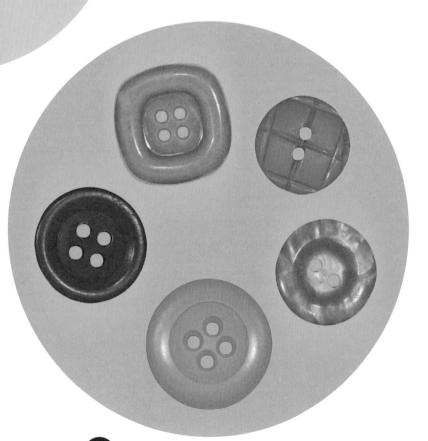

1
2
3
4
5
6
7
8
9
10

1
2
3
4
5
6
7
8
9
10

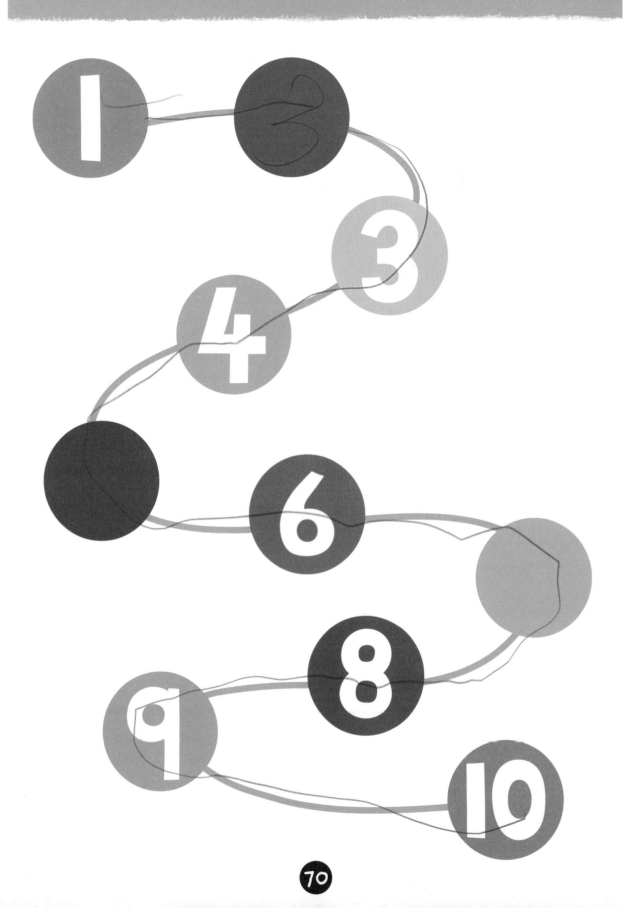

Add two sheep stickers to this field and draw **three** birds in the sky!

1
2
3
4
5
6
7
8
9
10

Use your stickers or crayons to add six cars and trucks to the road.

1
2
3
4
5
6
7
8
9
10

How many trees can you count on these pages?

1
2
3
4
5
6
7
8
9
10

1

2

3

4

5

6

7

8

9

10

Trace the numbers and color in the word names.

 **one**

 **two**

3 **three**

4 **four**

 **five**

6 six

7 seven

8 eight

9 nine

10 ten

1
2
3
4
5
6
7
8
9
10

Each number sentence adds up to ten. Find the missing sticker to finish the number sentence.

$1 + 9 = 10$

$2 + ? = 10$

$3 + ? = 10$

$4 + ? = 10$

$5 + ? = 10$

$6 + ? = 10$

$7 + ? = 10$

$8 + ? = 10$

$9 + ? = 10$

1
2
3
4
5
6
7
8
9
10

ANSWERS

Pages 8-9: There are two boats on the river. There are two helicopters in the sky.

Page 12: There are two shoes in each pair.

Page 14: There are three goldfish in the bowl.

Page 21: There are four party hats and four party blowers.

Page 26: You have five fingers.

Page 29: There are five flowers.

Page 33: There are six buns.

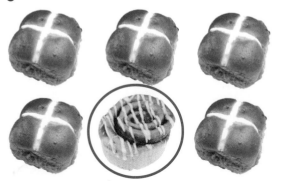

Page 38: There are seven ballet dancers on the stage.

Page 44: There are eight gold coins in the treasure chest.

Pages 46-47: There are eight stars.

Page 50:

Pages 58-59:

Fido

Fluff

ANSWERS

Fifi

Ferdy

Fred

Fonzy

Fizz

Finn

Flo

Floppy

Page 60: The gloves have ten fingers and thumbs in total.

Page 64: 2+3=5; 4+1=5; 3+4=7

Pages 68-69: There are three feathers. There are four crayons. There are six eggs. There are two gloves. There are five buttons.

Page 70:

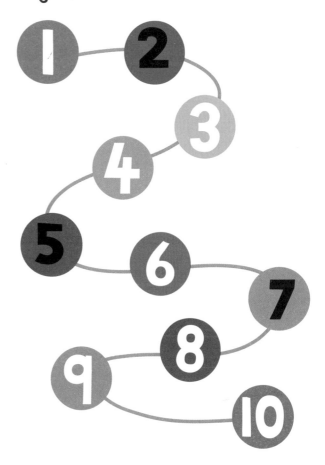

Pages 72-73: There are four trees on the page.

Pages 76-77: 2+8=10; 3+7=10; 4+6=10; 5+5=10; 6+4=10; 7+3=10; 8+2=10; 9+1=10.

1 2 3
4 5 6 7
8 9 10